SHORT TRAIN, LONG TRAIN

FRANK ASCH

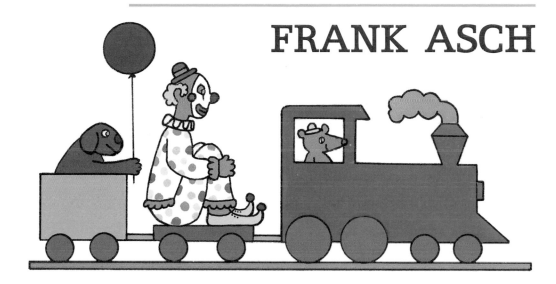

Cartwheel
·B·O·O·K·S·™

SCHOLASTIC INC.

NEW YORK TORONTO LONDON AUCKLAND SYDNEY

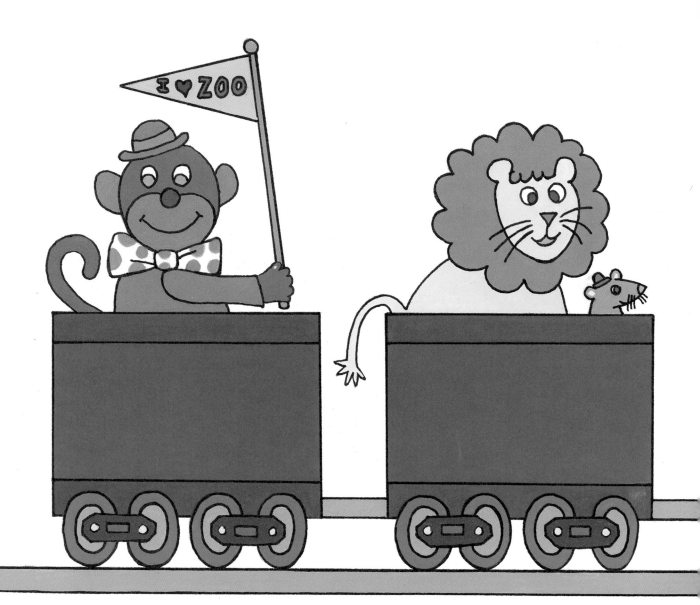

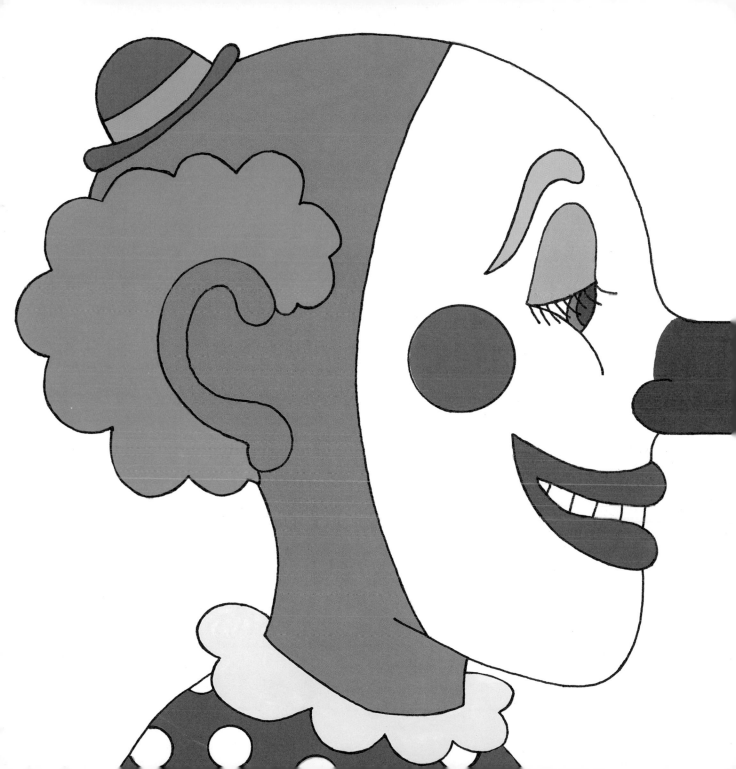

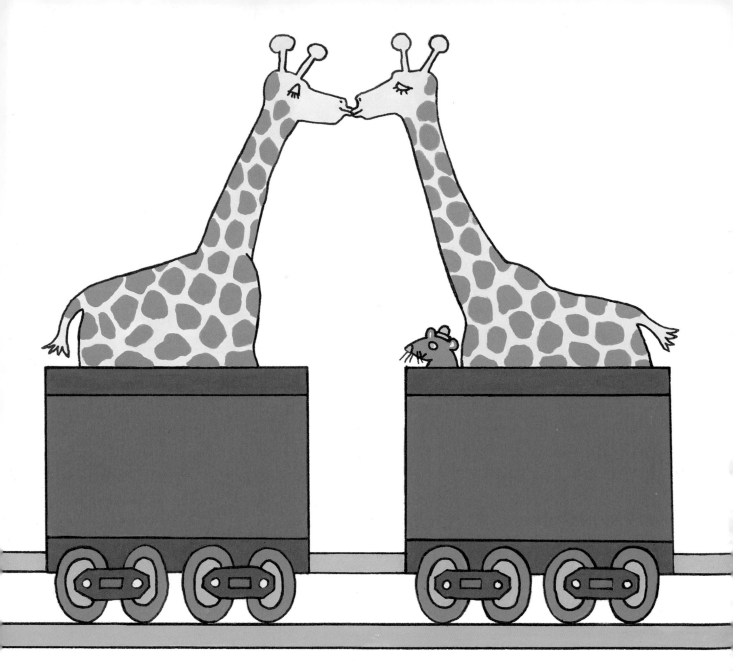

LONG TRAIN

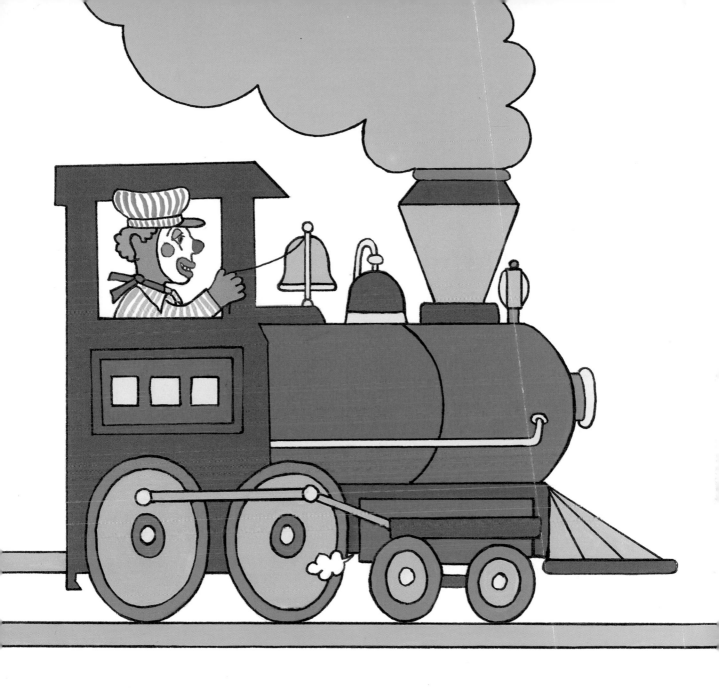

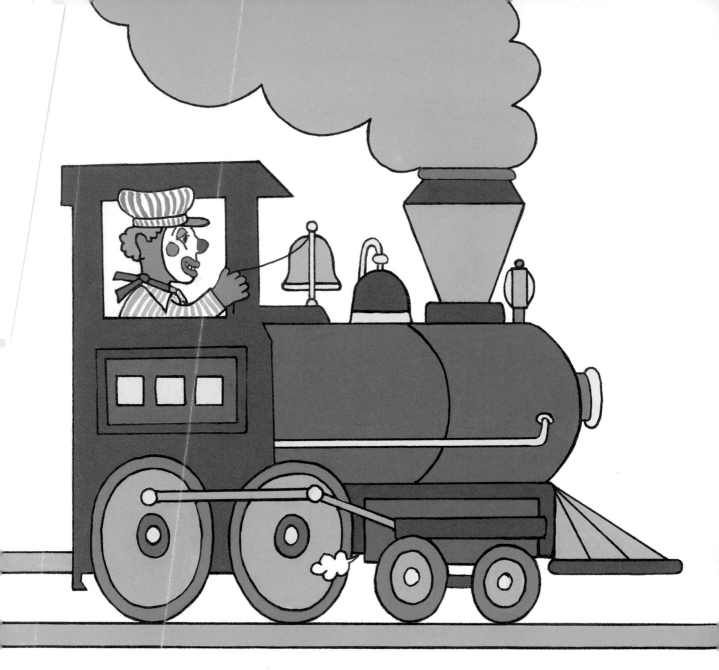

SHORT TRAIN

SHORT NOSE

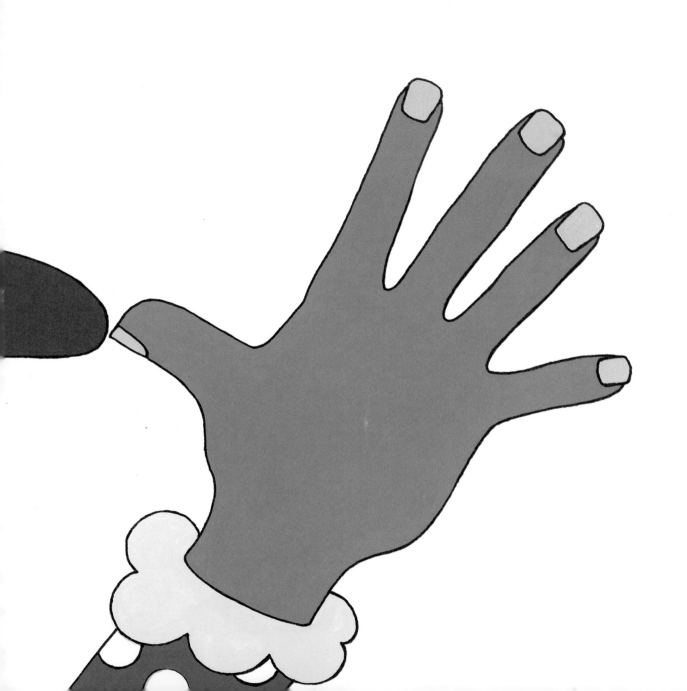

LONG NOSE

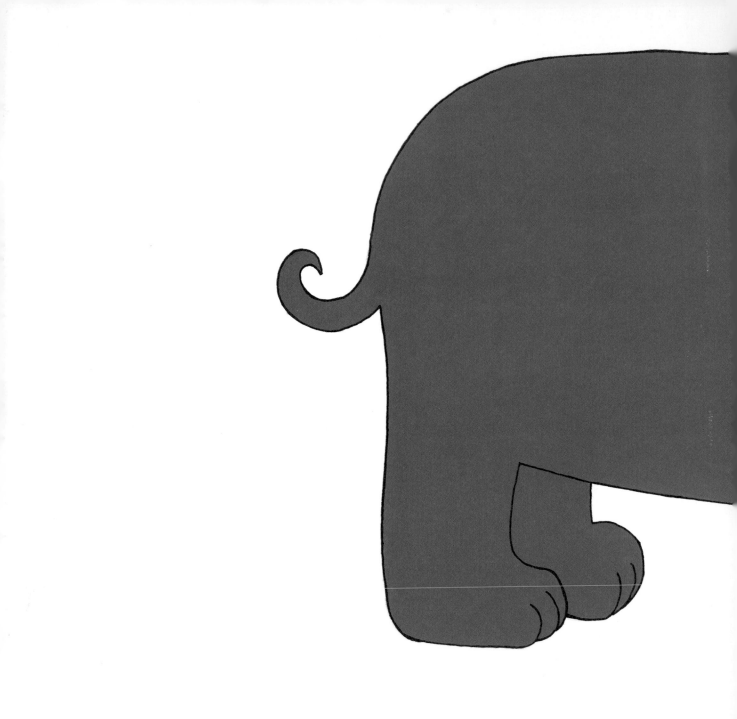

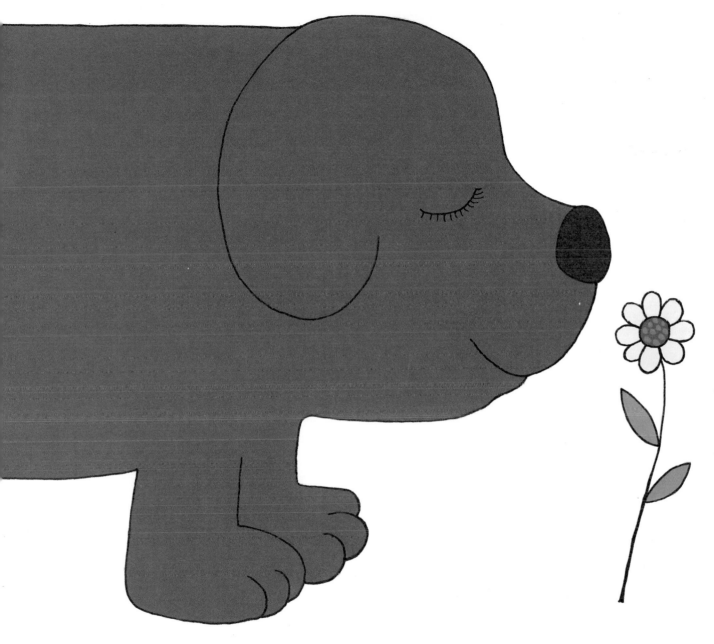

SHORT DOG

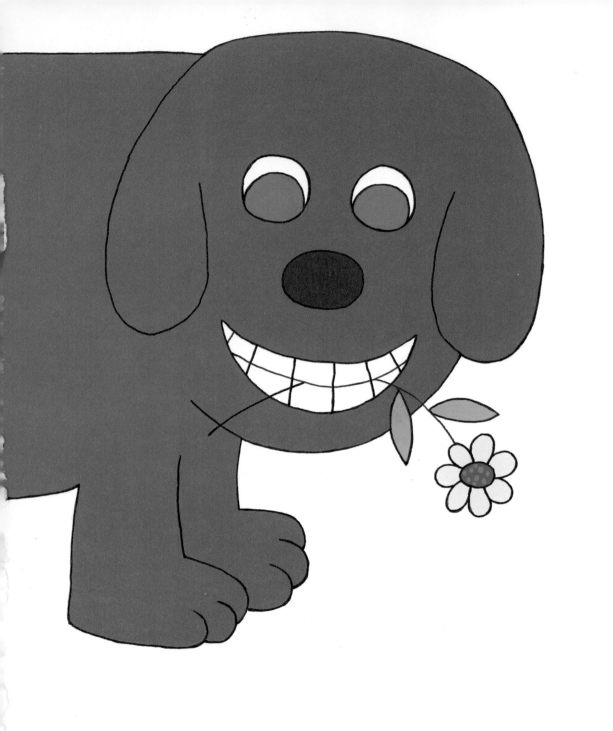

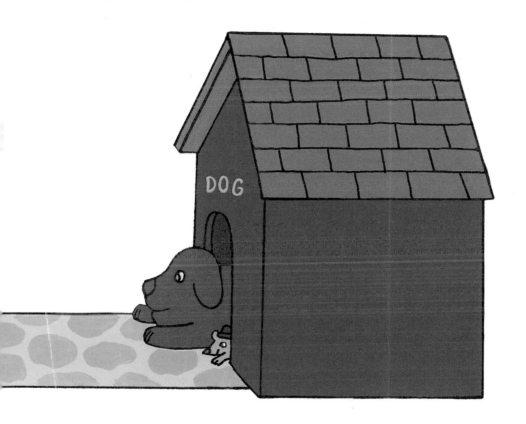

SHORT WALK

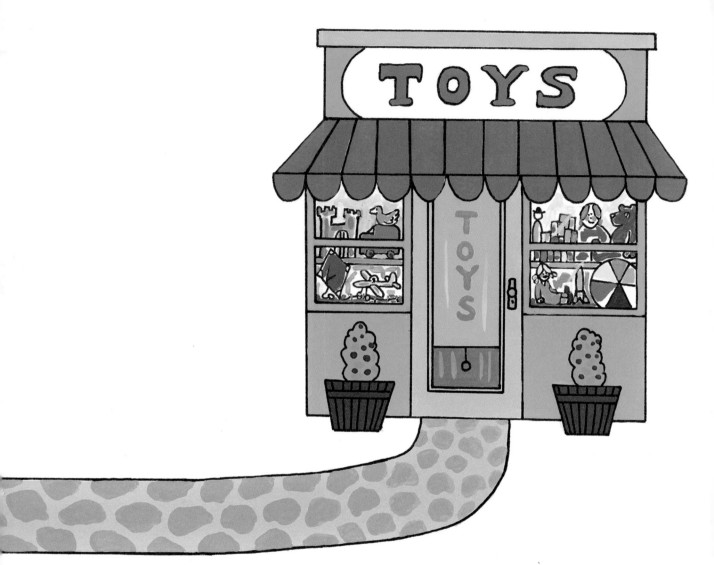

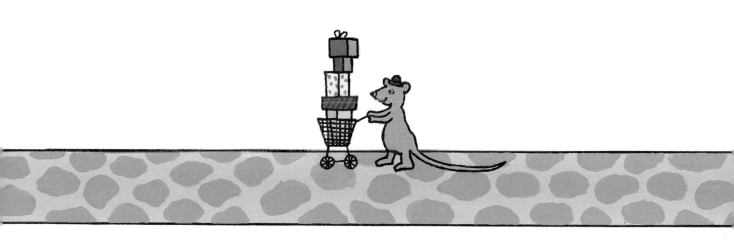

LONG WALK

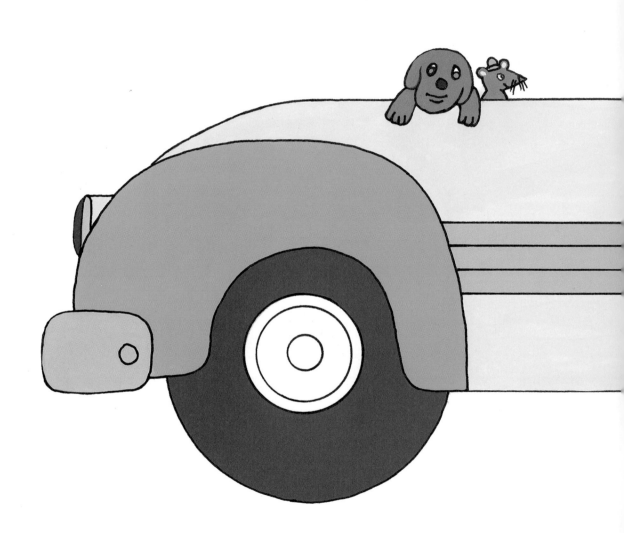

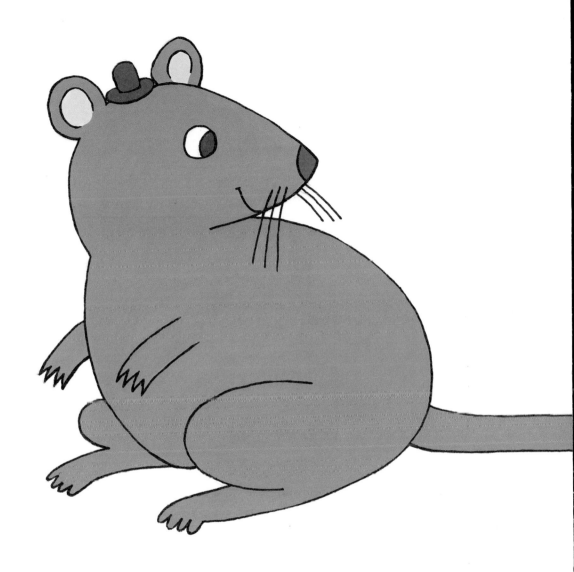

SHORT TAIL

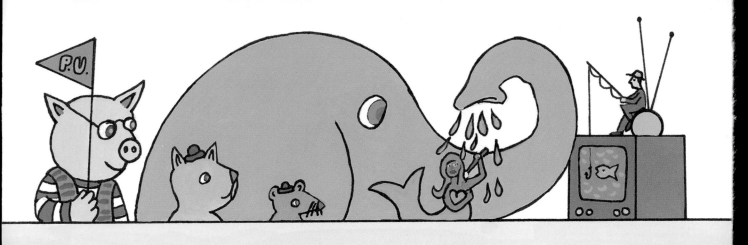

LONG CAR

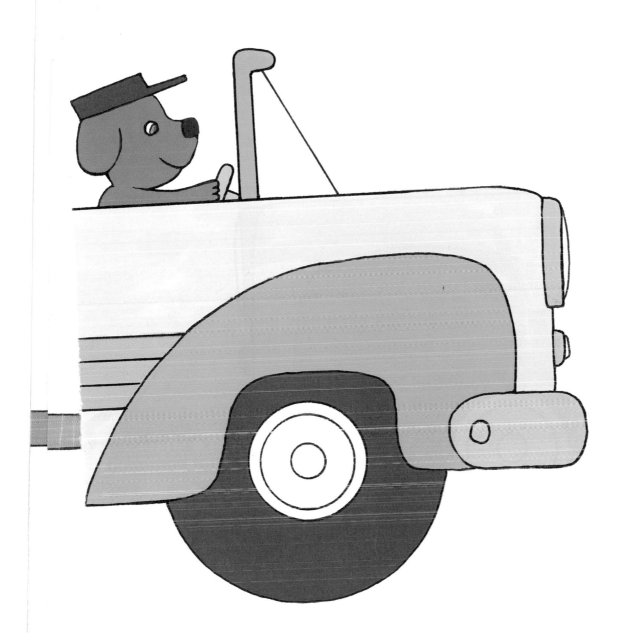